ROBERT BURLEIGH

HERCULES

ILLUSTRATED BY

RAUL COLÓN

SILVER WHISTLE
HARCOURT BRACE & COMPANY
SAN DIEGO NEW YORK LONDON

Library of Congress Cataloging-in-Publication Data
Burleigh, Robert.
Hercules/by Robert Burleigh; illustrated by Raúl Colón.
p. cm.
"Silver Whistle."
Summary: Retells the story of the final, and most difficult, labor of Hercules, known as Heracles in Greek mythology,
in which he must go to the Underworld and bring back the three-headed dog, Cerberus.
ISBN 0-15-201667-8
1. Hercules (Roman mythology)—Juvenile literature. 2. Heracles (Greek mythology)—Juvenile literature.
3. Cerberus (Greek mythology)—Juvenile literature. [1. Heracles (Greek mythology). 2. Hercules (Roman mythology).
3. Mythology, Greek. 4. Mythology, Roman.] I. Colón, Raúl, ill. II. Title.
BL820.H5B87 1999
398.2'093802—dc21 98-4989

First edition
A C E F D B

PRINTED IN HONG KONG

The illustrations in this book were done in watercolor and colored pencil on paper.
The display type was set in Sophia.
The text type was set in Meridien.
Color separations by Bright Arts Ltd., Hong Kong
Printed by South China Printing Company, Ltd., Hong Kong
This book was printed on totally chlorine-free Nymolla Matte Art paper.
Production supervision by Stanley Redfern and Ginger Boyer
Designed by Linda Lockowitz

For Charley and Kelsey Hill
—R. B.

For Hector
—R. C.

THE STORY OF HERCULES REFERS TO MANY CHARACTERS AND PLACES. THEY INCLUDE:

Athena—the Greek goddess of wisdom, war, and handicrafts

Black Sea—a large sea surrounded by Europe and Asia

Cerberus—the huge three-headed dog that guards Hades, the Greek Underworld

Charon—the man who ferries the dead across the River Styx and into Hades

Gorgon—a monster with snakes for hair whose gaze could turn all who looked upon it to stone

Hera—the sister and wife of Zeus

Iolaus—nephew and companion of Hercules

King Hades—god and ruler of the Underworld

King Rhadamanthus—the judge of the dead souls in the Underworld

Mount Olympus—the mountain in Greece where the ancient gods were said to live

Persephone—the wife of King Hades (he kidnapped her and brought her to the Underworld)

River Styx—a river in Hades, across which Charon ferries the souls of the dead

Sisyphus—a deceitful king, condemned forever to roll a stone up a hill in Hades

Zeus—the foremost Greek god and father of all the other gods and mortal heroes

FOREWORD

Hercules (the Roman name for the Greek hero Heracles) was one of the greatest of the legendary heroes of ancient Greece. He was famous for many reasons, including his twelve labors. These were twelve impossibly difficult tasks he had to complete so that Hera, the wife of the great god Zeus, would let him be free to live his own life. Hera was an enemy of Hercules' mother, and she took her anger out on the son. It took Hercules eight years to finish his labors. Many years later, he went to Mount Olympus to live with the gods.

He stands in front of an opening
Between two huge rocks,
As the sun sets over the shore
Of the Black Sea.
He looks back and waves to Iolaus:
Good-bye, good-bye, dear friend.
Then he turns.
Here is where no living human has ever gone.
This is the place, he thinks.
And I must go there.
I am afraid.
But also—I am not afraid.
For I am Hercules.

He enters the mouth of the cave.
Gone, swallowed by the doorway.
Hercules pauses to let his eyes sense the darkness.
For a moment, he recalls everything.
He remembers all his labors:
The long days and the hard nights,
The terror, and the courage.

He remembers killing the savage lion,
Whose magic pelt he now wears.
He remembers destroying the hydra with nine heads.
He remembers traveling to the end of the earth
To return with the golden apples.
He remembers escaping from the army of fierce women—the Amazons.
He remembers these things and more.

But now this.
He must endure this.
The last and most difficult labor:
To snare the fierce and fiery Cerberus.
To bring back the monster dog that guards the Underworld.
To return to the light with this most evil creature.
To go where the dead go—
And come back alive!

Raising his torch,
He reads words chiseled into the scarred wall:

WHO COMES TO THIS PLACE RETURNS BUT NEVER;
WHO DESCENDS NOW DESCENDS FOREVER.

WHO COMES TO
THIS PLACE
RETURNS BUT NEVER
WHO DESCENDS NOW
DESCENDS FOREVER

A chill flutters through Hercules' bones,
Yet down the stone steps he tiptoes.
Will Athena, the goddess of
Wisdom and bravery,
The goddess who loves him like a son,
Help him as she has before?
"Be with me now, blessed Athena,"
He whispers,
And thinks he hears a voice from
Somewhere answering.
"Be brave, Hercules," it says. "Be brave."

At the bottom of the stairs a river flows
By a rock wall.
The dead souls, who must pay to cross,
Flit back and forth like ghosts
Near the water's edge.
An evil-faced man wearing a cloak
Stands by a battered raft:
It is Charon,
Ferryman of the River Styx.

Charon holds out his hand for money,
But Hercules shakes his head.
"I am from the living," he says boldly.
"I am alive.
Expect nothing from me."
Their eyes clash and Hercules raises his club.
But the ferryman backs away
And points to the raft.
Together they walk toward it.

Soundlessly,
They push into the river.
And the rocky bank fades behind them.

On the far side of the river,
Hercules follows a narrow winding road.
How strange it is, he says to himself.
No flowers grow here.
No birds sing in the trees.

The great palace of King Hades looms up.
Its high spires, carved from pure black marble,
Shine with a gloomy, dark glow.
Hercules tiptoes to the wall,
Jumps up, clings, climbs, and peers down.

He sees a beautiful girl in a garden.
He knows it is Persephone, the sad queen.
She was kidnapped long ago and carried to this lightless place.
Tears fall from her eyes.
And there, walking silently behind her,
Is the somber king of the Underworld himself:
Hades!

Hercules cringes,
But cries out from the top of the wall,
"Hear me, Hades.
I am Hercules.
I have come to take the monster dog of the Underworld.
I come to bring back fearful Cerberus."

Hades looks up, glowers, laughs.
"Take him, Hercules,"
He calls back with an icy voice.
"He is yours—if you can take him
With nothing more than your two bare hands!
Ha, ha, ha!"

With only his hands!
There is no turning back.
So close to the end of his labors!
Hercules, the chill laughter still ringing
In his ears,
Jumps to the ground.

He speeds through the dim light.
His feet, moving here and then there,
Somehow know the way.
Is the goddess nearby?
Athena?
He races on, past towering boulders
And deep smoking pits that stare up
Like reddish eyes.

He runs past King Rhadamanthus,
Who judges the dead.
He runs past the high hill where
Pitiful Sisyphus
Pushes his heavy rock till the end of time.
He runs past the horrible witchlike Gorgon,
Whose gaze can turn men to granite.

Suddenly—by the bank of a river—
Hercules halts.
An instinct tells him,
Stop here.
This is the place. This is it.
He lays down his club.
He stands absolutely still.
He listens.
He waits.

He squints toward where
A low growling sound rises out of the mist.
Very slowly, a shape begins to form.
Before his eyes
Appears a massive dog with three heads—
Each head covered with hissing snakes—
And a tail pointed and jagged like a powerful spear.
Cerberus!
Cerberus at last!

They circle each other
Through ribbons of cold fog:
Hercules, Cerberus.
The three mouths snarl and the dog charges.
"Be strong, Hercules!" He hears Athena's voice call.
Hercules dives to one side,
Somersaults into the clear,
And bounds to his feet.

Again the dog crouches—and springs.
It flails with its spiked tail.
But the beast's attack fails.

Round and round and around.
Growls and heaves and cries.
A death dance in the valley of the dead.
Cerberus hesitates and Hercules sees his opening.
With two rapid strides
He reaches the dog-beast.
His fingers clutch the rippling neck from behind.
One head turns and teeth fasten to his pelted arm.

Hands clench and fangs bite down in the final struggle.
Man and monster,
Monster and man.

Hercules feels the dog's bite slacken.
The high-pitched howls
Become whimpers and then whines.
The great beast's thick legs go limp.
It tumbles over, twists, and moans.

Cerberus is defeated.
Hercules is victorious.

Hercules drags the captured animal through
The foul-smelling water.
He once more finds the passageway.
Up, up, and up.
The dog chained tightly behind him,
Hercules climbs with his last strength toward
A glowing ray of light.

Ah, the sun, the sun!
But Cerberus, hauled from his dark underground house,
Thrashes against the sudden brightness,
Black foam dripping from his lips.

Iolaus wheels the chariot to the cave's entrance.
Seeing the huge dog flung into the chariot,
The horses squeal and shy back, pawing at the air.
But Iolaus holds hard to the reins and heads for home.

The gates of the city swing open.

Hercules, free at last,
Raises his captive into the air.
The people stare in wonder, shouting:
"Hercules.
Hercules.
Hercules."

Alone, in the calm of the evening,
Hercules sits under an old olive tree.
So many years, he thinks to himself.
So many journeys.
And yet—the day is good.
The night is good.
The goddess Athena is good.
My labors are finished, never to be forgotten.
O I have done what I feared I could not do.
I, Hercules.